For my sons Sebastian and Benedikt,
who know that I am always there
for them—PH

First published in the United States, Great Britain, Canada,
Australia, and New Zealand in 2003 by North-South Books,
an imprint of NordSüd Verlag AG, Gossau Zürich, Switzerland.
First paperback edition published in 2005 by North-South Books.
Distributed in the United States by North-South Books Inc., New York.

Library of Congress Cataloging-in-Publication Data
Horn, Peter.
The best father of all / Peter Horn; illustrated by Cristina Kadmon;
translated by J. Alison James.
p. cm.
Summary: A turtle father and son play a guessing game about what kind
of father does certain things for his children, such as chirping encouragement
as they learn to fly, or organizing a croaking concert.
[1. Fathers—Fiction. 2. Parental behavior in animals—Fiction.
3. Turtles—Fiction. 4. Animals—Fiction.]
I. Kadmon, Cristina, ill. II. James, J. Alison. III. Title.
PZ7.H78225 Be 2003 [E]—dc21 2002007816A

A CIP catalogue record for this book is available from The British Library.

ISBN 0-7358-1679-4 (trade edition)
3 5 7 9 HC 10 8 6 4
ISBN 0-7358-1680-8 (library edition)
1 3 5 7 9 LE 10 8 6 4 2
ISBN 0-7358-1977-7 (paperback edition)
1 3 5 7 9 PB 10 8 6 4 2
Printed in Belgium

For more information about our books, and the authors and artists
who create them, visit our web site: www.northsouth.com

The Best Father of All

By Peter Horn • Illustrated by Cristina Kadmon

Translated by J. Alison James

North-South Books

New York • London

It was a lovely autumn day. The leaves of the trees rustled in the cool wind.

Sebastian the little turtle sat by his father in the grass. "I feel so safe when I'm with you," said Sebastian.

"That's what a father does," said his father. "He keeps you safe."

"What else does a father do?" asked Sebastian.

"Well, a father encourages his children. He chirps to them when they try to fly for the first time. Can you guess which father that is?"

"I know!" said Sebastian. "A father bird!"

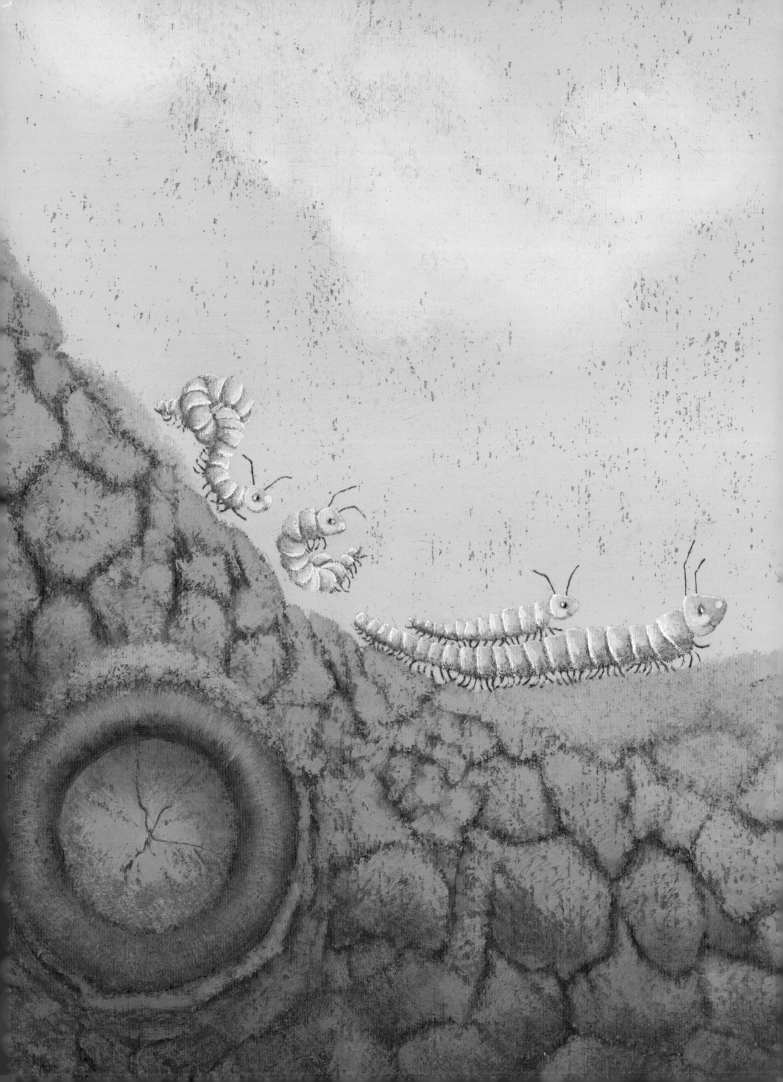

"A father untangles hundreds of legs when his children stumble," said Father.

"That's a father centipede!" cried Sebastian.

"A father teaches his children to spring and bounce in the grass," said Father.

"That must be a father rabbit," said Sebastian. "What else does a father do?"

"A father shows his children how to hop from stalk to stalk in the cornfield," said Father.

"That's a father grasshopper!" cried Sebastian.

"A father explains how to spin webs that glitter with dew in the early morning."

Sebastian knew that father right away. "A father spider!" he declared.

"A father organizes croaking concerts, so all the animals on the pond can hear his children's fine voices."

"That's a father frog!" cried Sebastian. "What else does a father do?"

"A father sticks berries on his spikes and carries them to his children when they are hungry from playing and rolling about," said Father.

"That has to be the funny father hedgehog," said Sebastian, laughing.

"Now this one is difficult," said Father to Sebastian. "A father puts his children to sleep in the middle of the day. He teaches them to hang by their toes from a branch."

Sebastian thought for a moment, then he said, "That must be a father bat."

"Well done!" said Father. "Can you guess which father flies with his children, making wonderful loops of light?"

"That is a father firefly," Sebastian declared. "What else does a father do?"

"A father plays hide-and-seek with his son and slides with him down the dewy wet grass.

"A father helps his son flip over on his legs when he is stuck upside-down on his shell.

"A father enjoys a bite with his son when the strawberries are ripe and juicy.

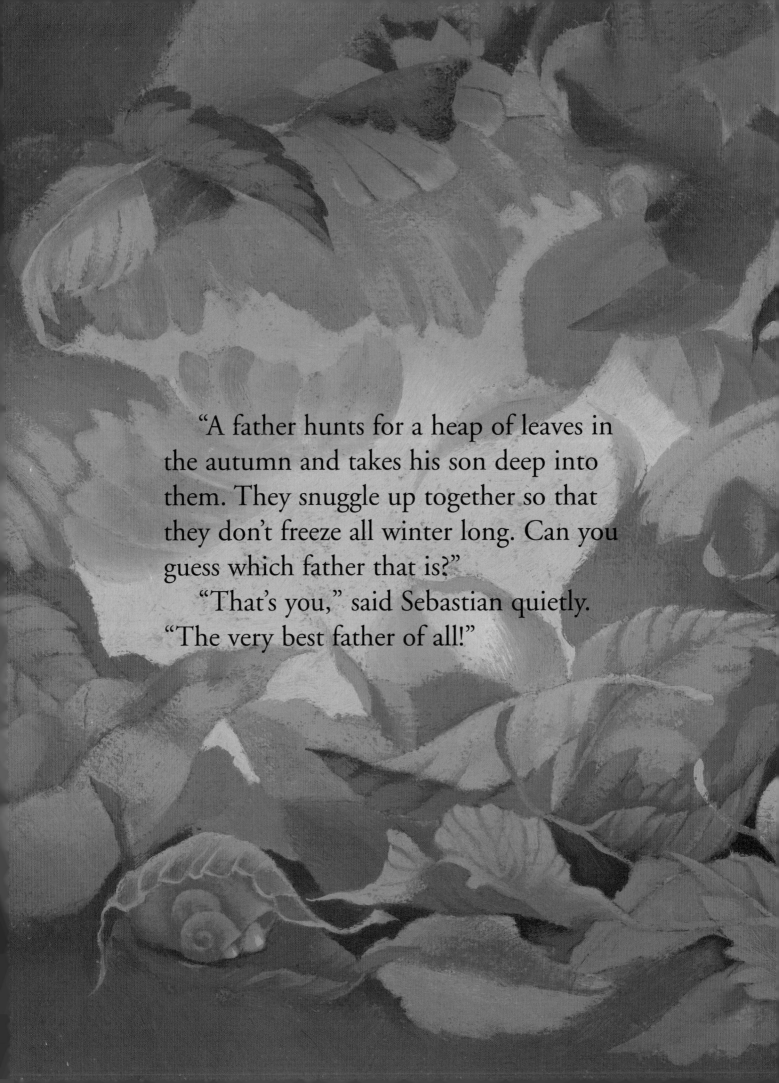

"A father hunts for a heap of leaves in the autumn and takes his son deep into them. They snuggle up together so that they don't freeze all winter long. Can you guess which father that is?"

"That's you," said Sebastian quietly. "The very best father of all!"